Dorkius Maximus
IN POMPEII

DIARY OF
Dorkius Maximus
IN POMPEII

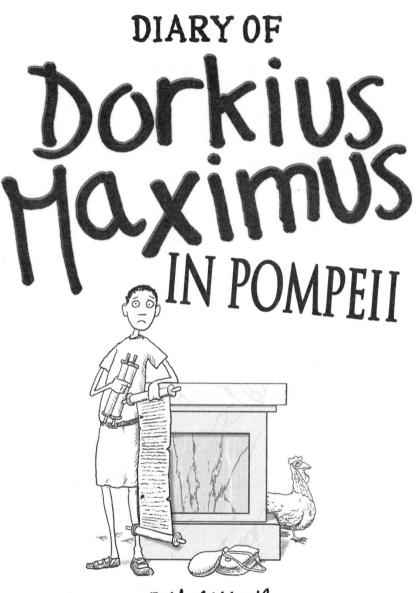

TIM COLLINS

BUSTER

Written by Tim Collins
Illustrated by Andrew Pinder

Edited by Sophie Schrey and Philippa Wingate
Cover design by Angie Allison

First published in Great Britain in 2014 by Buster Books,
an imprint of Michael O'Mara Books Limited,
9 Lion Yard, Tremadoc Road, London SW4 7NQ

www.busterbooks.co.uk

A CIP catalogue record for this book is available
from the British Library.

ISBN: 978-1-78055-268-2 in paperback print format
ISBN: 978-1-78055-276-7 in ebook format

1 3 5 7 9 10 8 6 4 2

Papers used by Michael O'Mara Books are natural,
recyclable products made from wood grown in sustainable forests.
The manufacturing processes conform to the environmental
regulations of the country of origin.

Printed and bound in May 2014 by CPI Group (UK) Ltd,
108 Beddington Lane, Croydon, CR0 4YY, United Kingdom.

Acknowledgements

Thanks to Sophie Schrey, Bryony Jones,
Philippa Wingate, Hannah Cohen, Andrew Pinder,
Hilary Stroh, Nick Hurley and Collette Collins.

Mum and Dad

Pontius and Pullo, magistrates from Pompeii

Decima, my only friend in Pompeii

Mum's sacred chickens, my new roommates

THIS DIARY BELONGS TO: DORKIUS MAXIMUS AGED: 13 YEARS SOMETIMES a Roman hero (honest!)

My best friend in Rome, Linos

Servius, mad soothsayer who makes pathetic predictions

Marcus, my so-called teacher

Spurius, forgetful man whose job it is to remember names

MAP OF POMPEII

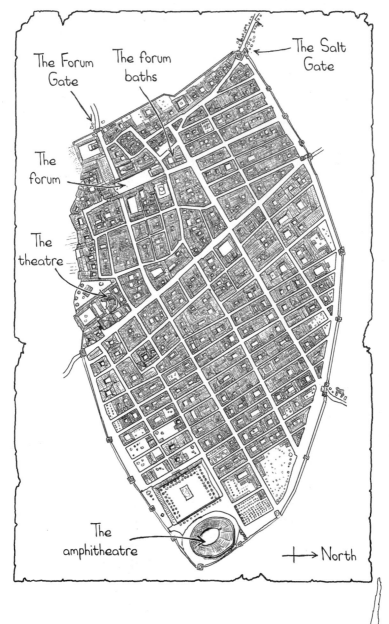

The Forum Gate

The forum baths

The Salt Gate

The forum

The theatre

The amphitheatre

North

June 1

Disaster! We're all leaving Rome for the summer and going to some miserable little town that's miles away. Who would be crazy enough to leave Rome, the GREATEST city in the world, for Pompeii, a dump no one's ever heard of? My dad, that's who.

Mum's not sure she wants to go either. I don't usually listen to her bonkers superstitions, but Servius, her soothsayer, has made a useful prediction for once.

A mighty roar will split the earth. Fire will flow and rocks will fall. Slaves, freedmen and citizens will be buried side by side.

But does Dad listen to me or the soothsayer? NO.

June 11

Mum is still fretting about going to Pompeii but Dad won't give in. Julius Caesar has ordered him to make the local government pay more tax, and you don't argue with Caesar if you like having your head on your body.

Okay, Caesar. I admit I was wrong.

Mum won't stop moaning, so Dad put our slave Odius on listening duty tonight. All Odius had to do was sit there while Mum went on about how terrible it would be if we moved to Pompeii. But after half an hour he gave up, saying he remembered he had to scrub the atrium.

Odius usually LOVES sitting around doing nothing. At least we know how to make him work now.

Tidy the kitchen or I'll make you listen to my wife.

June III

This is VERY suspicious. Mum came back from seeing Servius today and announced she wants to go to Pompeii after all. Apparently, Servius read some new pig entrails and changed his prophecy.

A light breeze will blow across the earth. Excellent wine will flow and wonderful food will be served. Slaves, freedmen and citizens will all have a lovely summer.

I asked Dad if he'd bribed the greedy old soothsayer, but he denied it. Yet this afternoon I spotted Servius in the market buying a bronze statue. Bit of a coincidence that he can afford such fancy stuff so soon after changing his prophecy, eh?

Just as I thought. The whole prophecy thing is COMPLETELY and UTTERLY pointless.

I predict your Dad'll hand over money to someone who doesn't know what he's talking about.

June IV

It gets worse. I just asked my best friend Linos if he wanted to come to Pompeii with me, but he said he's too busy with his wee laundry. He's become a real workaholic since he opened that place. He doesn't even pause for a toilet break, because he can just use the laundry tub he's standing in. It's quite an efficient system, really.

Fresh washing liquid

June V

I was planning to take my full set of gladiator figurines with me to Pompeii, but Dad said there wouldn't be room for them in the cart.

But guess what I saw when I clambered in? Mum's sacred chickens. So we've got room for THEM, have we?

Mum is obsessed with those chickens. The only way she can make any decisions is to ask their opinion by offering them grain. Apparently, she asked if they wanted to come, and they said yes, so she HAD to bring them.

I admit that the chickens didn't look much like they wanted to come, but are they really going to squawk for the whole journey?

Mum cares more about those chickens than about me. I'm surprised she didn't make me and Dad carry them on a litter.

June IX

We arrived in Pompeii as it was getting dark. We had to ride round a massive mountain called Vesuvius and down a road lined with graves to reach the town.

We entered the city by the Salt Gate and stopped in front of a bald man who was slouching on the floor and chewing a piece of bread. Dad asked him for directions to the house that had the mosaic of a guard dog outside it, but he just shrugged.

Caesar has arranged for us to stay in this house, and he assured us everyone would know where it was. Everyone except this man, apparently.

We trailed round the streets looking for the mosaic, only to arrive back where we'd started. The bald man was standing up now, and it turned out he'd been sitting on the mosaic of a guard dog.

When Dad asked him why he'd misled us, he said he couldn't understand our accents. Accents? We're the ones who sound normal. They're the ones who sound like weirdos.

Beware of the dog!

Beware of the unhelpful idiot!

CAVE CANEM

I've been given a small room at the side of the atrium and I'm currently lying on my bed and wondering how things could get any worse.

June X

Remind me NEVER to wonder how things can get worse. Soon after I'd written that last diary entry, Mum threw the sacred chickens into my room. When I asked her what she was doing, she said she'd placed grain outside each door to discover which room they wanted to stay in.

And guess what? They chose mine. Of COURSE they did.

Needless to say, I had a terrible night. Every time I drifted off to sleep, the chickens clucked in my ear and woke me up.

So I got up at first light and went out to see the town. I'd assumed the bit of town we rode round last night was the grotty

CLUCK CLUCK

part, but it turns out to have been the whole thing.

As I wandered about, a horrible fishy smell kept wafting into my nostrils. After a while, I worked out where it was coming from. It's this really stinky fish sauce they make here. Every stall sells it, and everyone drenches all their food in it. YUCK.

I thought things were looking up when Dad said we were having dormice for dinner.

But when our new chef stomped out of the kitchen and I saw he was that bald man who'd been slumped outside the house yesterday, my hopes fell.

No prizes for guessing which rancid sauce he smothered the dormice in. What a waste of a tasty treat.

June XI

Dad is just as annoyed with this place as I am. This morning he went out to look for the local government officials. He stopped to ask a group of layabouts in the forum if they knew where to find them. It turns out they WERE them.

He asked for a meeting, and they said he was already having one. It didn't turn out to be a very long one. When Dad asked them if they'd pay more tax, they refused.

It's all down to two magistrates called Pontius and Pullo. Dad said they were stubborn and stupid, and wouldn't listen to any of his promises or threats. I hope they change their minds soon. I can't stand it here.

June XII

Dad seems to think we'll be here for a while, because he sent me to the local school today to help me 'settle down'. I don't want to settle down, I want to go home.

He took me to a tiny building near the forum and pulled back a curtain to reveal a small room with red walls and two rows of pupils facing a teacher.

'Hi, I'm Dorkius Maximus from Rome,' I said, taking my place on one of the benches.

'I'm Marcus,' said the teacher. 'We're doing alphabet today. Let me know if you have trouble keeping up.'

I wondered what sort of lesson could possibly be called 'alphabet'. But as I settled down on my bench, my classmates warmed up by reciting every letter over and over again.

After half an hour, it dawned on me. This wasn't the warm up for the lesson. This WAS the lesson. And it went on and on and on.

Speaking as someone who's heard Mum talking to her sacred chickens for hours on end, I thought I knew boredom. But this was something else.

When it had FINALLY finished, the boy next to me said, 'I love alphabet. It's my favourite lesson. What's yours?'

I tried to think of what else might count as a lesson around here. Breathing? Going to the toilet? Staring at rocks?

'Public speaking,' I said.

The boy nodded thoughtfully, but I could tell he didn't have clue what I was on about. This is going to be a LONG summer.

June XIII

At least one of us is happy here. I came home this afternoon to find Mum showing her sacred chickens to a group of townsfolk who had gathered in the atrium.

Mum fed grain to the birds and explained how they were predicting the future. You'd think the locals had just discovered fire from the way they were staring in open-mouthed wonder.

When Mum finished, people lined up to toss grain at the chickens and ask them questions. A man at the back got really worried when he asked them if he'd have good fortune and they refused to eat the grain. I pointed out that the chickens had just eaten ten portions of grain, and they were just really full, but he ignored me.

The chickens were probably right, though. No one that stupid could have good fortune.

Why are you refusing the grain?

WHY?

June XIV

Marcus said we were going to have a
writing lesson today, and I assumed it
would be a little more challenging than the
alphabet lesson. I should have known better.
It consisted of nothing more than the pupils
writing their names on their wax tablets
over and over again.

Marcus told me to join in, so I took my
scroll, ink and quill out of my bag. There
were gasps all around the room as I began
to write.

I thought Marcus might think I was a genius
for being able to write more than my own
name, but he told me off for disrupting the
class with fancy things.

Fancy? This lot think scrolls are fancy? They

probably still think the wheel is cutting-edge technology.

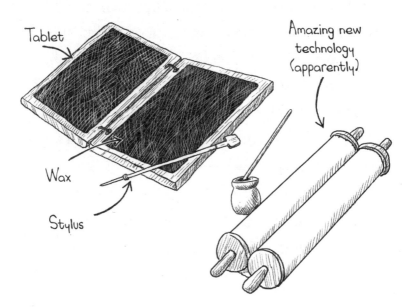

Tablet

Amazing new technology (apparently)

Wax

Stylus

The class gathered round as I explained how I write an account of everything that happens in my scroll. I tried to demonstrate by reading the entry about my first day in the class, but then I remembered I wasn't very nice about them, so I made up a more positive account instead.

The whole class applauded when I'd finished.

'I can't believe we've appeared in a scroll,' said the boy next to me. 'Wait until I tell Mum and Dad.'

I'm glad I made the account sound more positive. My classmates might be thick, but they seem nice, and it would have been a shame to upset them.

June XV

I made an effort to hang around with some of the boys from school today, but I didn't have much in common with them. I tried to get the conversation going by asking them what they want to be when they grow up.

'I want to be a litter carrier,' said one.
'You get to visit lots of different parts of
Pompeii and be near important people.'

'I want to be a floor cleaner,' said another.
'My uncle does that, and he finds loads of
coins people have dropped.'

'I want to be a wee collector,' said another. 'For the local laundry.'

'You're just a dreamer,' said the first one. 'No one from our school has ever got a job like that.'

'I have a friend who used to be a wee collector,' I said. 'He owns his own laundry now.'

The boys listened in awe as I told them about Linos's wee laundry. I decided to practise my speech-making skills by turning it into a rousing speech about how everyone should follow their dreams.

I can't believe the dream in question was wee collecting, though. Whatever happened to wanting to be a centurion or a senator or a chariot racer? These Pompeii kids need to aim a lot higher.

June XVI

Dad tried to send me back to school today, but I refused to go. I told him the lessons were actually making me stupider, and if I went to any more of them I'd forget how to eat and sit on chairs. He said he didn't want me moping around the house all day and went out to find me a tutor.

He soon returned and announced that the only tutor in Pompeii had left town over a month ago. He was called Numerius and he lived in the house opposite the Forum Gate. Apparently he was the cleverest man in the whole of Pompeii, but that isn't saying much. It's like being the nicest-smelling worker in the wee laundry.

Dad says no one knows why he left. Er ... let me guess. Is it because this entire town is full of dimwits? It's more of a mystery that a smart man like Numerius wanted to live here in the first place.

Pompeii's cleverest resident

Pompeii's second cleverest resident

June XVII

I was walking past the Forum Gate today when I saw Numerius's house and I decided to have a snoop. I was hoping he might have left some empty scrolls behind that I could 'borrow', but I couldn't find any. One of the rooms was lined with narrow shelves. It must have been an impressive library once.

I noticed someone had scratched the words, 'Fortune looks over cold water', into one of the shelves, but it didn't mean anything to me. It seemed a very strange piece of graffiti. People usually write about how horrible their ex-girlfriends are or what a satisfying poo they've just had. They don't write nonsense phrases like that.

I'm guessing Numerius wrote it. Given that everyone else around here seems to have trouble writing their own names, it's quite likely. But why? Was it a secret clue to something? I can't work it out.

Name-spelling FAIL

June XVIII

Pontius and Pullo called round this afternoon, followed by a large group of slaves.

'Excellent,' said Dad, striding into the atrium. 'Does this mean you've reconsidered the whole tax situation?'

'No,' said Pontius. 'We're here to see these amazing chickens we've heard so much about.'

Dad tutted and stormed back into his room.

They crouched down and inspected the birds. Mum came in with a handful of grain and began her usual demonstration of their so-called magical powers.

Pontius and Pullo watched in amazement.

THE INCREDIBLE
GRAIN-EATING
CHICKENS

I can't believe those are the people Dad has to persuade to pay more tax. They're IDIOTS. We'll be stuck here forever.

'Hello, I'm Spurius,' said one of the slaves, who came over and shook my hand. 'I'm a nomenclator, which means it's my job to remember the names and details of everyone in town so my masters don't have to. It helps save embarrassment.'

'I'm Dorkius Maximus,' I said. 'And I'm a true Roman hero.' Spurius nodded.

When Pontius and Pullo were leaving, Spurius pointed at me and said, 'That's Doofus Maximus. True Roman weirdo.' Pontius and Pullo smiled at me.

I couldn't believe it. His only job is to remember names and he forgot mine after just a few minutes.

And these are the sacred pigeons.

June XIX

There was a gladiator show in the local amphitheatre today, and I went along because I thought it might cheer me up.

The amphitheatre was surprisingly impressive, though the corridors smelt like Linos's laundry. It was packed with thousands of supporters, so I thought I was in for a great afternoon of gory fun.

Half the crowd were chanting 'Celadus' and the other half were chanting 'Cresces'. I'd never heard either name before, but reckoned they must be good fighters to get everyone so worked up.

I knew I couldn't be more wrong as soon as I saw the gladiators coming out from opposite sides of the arena and wheezing across the sand. Celadus had a small sword and a rusty helmet, while Cresces had a tatty net and a bent trident.

Neither of them looked like the fighters I watch in Rome. They were fat and looked at least ten years too old for the job.

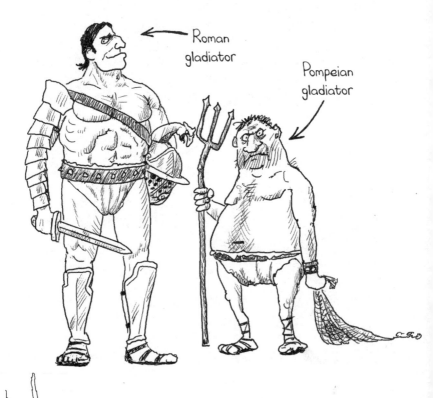

← Roman gladiator

Pompeian gladiator

In fact, Celadus had to stop and get his breath back before he'd even reached the middle of the arena. Rather than charging in for the kill, Cresces took his helmet off and scratched his head, revealing thinning grey hair.

When they finally got round to fighting, it wasn't hard to see why gladiators live to be so old around here. They jabbed weakly at each other, bumbling back and forth. The only thing they were likely to die of was old age.

Not that you'd have known from the reaction of the crowd. They gasped and cheered. I tried to explain to the man next to me how much better gladiator battles are back in Rome, but he got up and moved away. So did the man next to him, and the next man along. I didn't care, because I ended up with practically a whole row to myself.

After a few minutes, Celadus threw himself to the floor and Cresces plonked a foot on his chest. And that was it. The 'entertainment' was over.

Back home, it would have been time to release some animals and have an awesome beast battle, but they didn't bother with anything like that. It's hardly surprising. Those two couldn't even fight a kitten.

MEH

June XX

I was passing the Temple of Fortuna Augusta this afternoon when I noticed the forum baths right opposite. This seemed important to me for some reason, but I couldn't put my finger on it. Then I remembered the words I'd seen scratched into the shelf in Numerius's house: 'Fortune looks over cold water.'

The baths have a cold-water pool. What if Numerius left the words as a secret clue for someone clever like me to discover? I rushed into the baths to investigate.

There was nobody in the pool and the water was so filthy it would make you dirtier instead of cleaner. As my eyes adjusted to the gloom, I noticed tiny letters etched into the rim of the pool. I leaned over the edge to examine them.

GO FROM COLD TO HOT,
WHERE THE BLIND BEAST CIRCLES.

My heart raced. Another clue! Numerius must have hidden something really important to go to all this effort.

I heard footsteps approaching and jumped with fright. Unfortunately, this made me plop into the pool and I surfaced in time to see Pontius and Spurius wandering through.

'This is Doltus Maximus,' said Spurius. 'He bathes with his clothes on because he's a true Roman weirdo.'

Pontius smiled and nodded and made his way through to the next pool. I waited in the cold water until he'd gone, then went outside to dry off.

I can't BELIEVE I've uncovered another secret clue. If only I had the slightest idea what it meant, I'd be even more excited.

June XXI

'Go from cold to hot, where the blind beast circles.'

To be honest, I'm getting nowhere with the new clue.

You could go from the cold pool to the hot pool in the baths, I suppose. But what would the 'blind beast' be? Some sort of eyeless sea monster? I know the public baths are

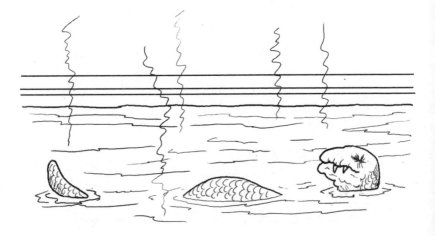

dirty, but surely someone would notice if a blind beast lived in the bottom.

It's worth investigating, I suppose.

UPDATE

I just checked the hot pool and didn't see any circling sea creatures. I saw Pontius lurking in the water, and he looks a bit like a monster. But he wasn't circling and Numerius couldn't have known he'd be there at the exact time I was looking.

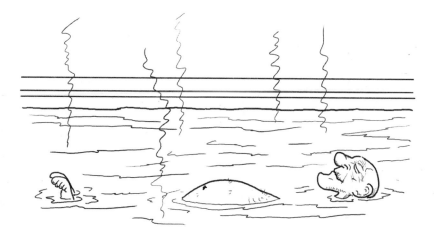

June XXII

I was lying awake last night trying to work out the answer to the clue I'd found at the baths, when I came up with a much better idea. I invented a FOOLPROOF plan to get Pontius and Pullo to agree to the tax demands so we can leave Pompeii for good.

I was thinking about how fascinated they were by the sacred chickens when I had my idea ...

Here it is: Mum invites Pontius and Pullo round and tells them to ask the chickens if Pompeii should pay the extra tax. In the meantime, we've starved the chickens, so they're bound to eat anything. When the chickens gobble the grain, Pontius and Pullo agree to the changes. We go home and I'm watching proper gladiators again in no time.

UPDATE
Dad loves my plan and Mum has invited
Pontius and Pullo round tomorrow. This
can't fail.

June XXIII

Pontius and Pullo came round this afternoon,
followed by Spurius, who pointed at me and
said, 'Dorkius Maximumass, weird Roman boy.'

They agreed to consult the chickens about the tax as soon as it was suggested, which proves they COULD pay if they chose to.

Pontius crouched down next to the chickens and asked, 'Should we agree to the new tax demands?'

Mum threw a handful of grain at the chickens, and I waited for them to start scoffing like crazy.

Sure enough, the chickens rushed towards it, but then they backed off.

'Come on,' I said. 'Get that lovely grain down your beaks.'

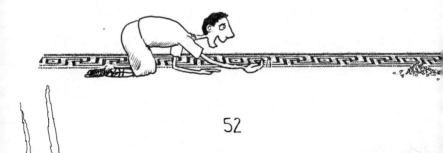

Instead of gobbling, the chickens fled to the opposite side of the atrium. I couldn't believe it. I'd been watching them all day to make sure they didn't eat. Why weren't they hungry?

'It looks like we have our answer,' said Pullo.

'Thanks, chickens,' said Pontius. 'Your decision shall be final.' And with that, they all sauntered out.

Dad glared at me. 'So much for your plan, Dorkius,' he shouted.

'It's not my fault,' I said. 'Blame those stupid chickens.'

'Don't be rude about the chickens,' said Mum. 'I'm sure they did it for a reason.'

'What has happened?' asked the chef, strolling in from the kitchen and glancing down at the grain on the floor. 'Didn't the chickens like my new grain recipe? I mixed some delicious fish sauce in, to make it nicer for them.'

AARRGH! My plan has failed and I'm trapped here all because of that stupid chef. Why did he think chickens loved eating fish? Has he seen them popping out on fishing trips?

June XXIV

This afternoon I heard Mum's new friends going on about a demon that supposedly lives on Mount Vesuvius.

Apparently, they've heard it growling, and sometimes it stomps around so heavily it makes the buildings shake all the way down here in Pompeii.

They're terrified the demon is going to come down and destroy the town, and they want the gods to shoo it away.

I peered out into the atrium and noticed Pontius and Pullo were among Mum's visitors. If even the town leaders are spouting this nonsense, what chance has anyone else got of keeping a level head?

Pullo crouched down next to one of the chickens and asked, 'How do we get the gods to chase the mountain demon away?'

What was he playing at? That's not how sacred chickens work. They can only give you 'yes' or 'no' answers, not detailed advice.

Pullo stood up again. 'They say we should make a sacrifice to appease the gods. Then they will send the demon away.'

Unfortunately, it wasn't the chickens Pullo had in mind for sacrificing. All Mum's bonkers visitors hurried away to the market to buy a cow, wasting money that could be spent paying the extra tax Dad needs.

UPDATE

I've just had a horrible nightmare about being bitten by a demon. I woke up and found one of the chickens was pecking my head.

I'll never get back to sleep now. I know there's no such thing as a mountain demon, but it's difficult not to worry when every shadow looks like a twisted, snarling monster.

Having said that, it might not be such a terrible thing if a demon DID turn up and eat the town, as long as we survived. At least we'd be allowed to go back home.

June XXV

I was desperate for the toilet on my way back from school today so I had to use the public loos. I usually hate them, because you have to go right in front of everyone else. But thankfully I found some that were totally deserted.

I was just about to go when Pontius and Spurius came in. I tried to look away but Spurius pointed right in my direction and said, 'Dullus Maximus, Roman weirdo.'

Pontius nodded at me, sat down and started using the toilet. I can't believe even the leaders of this shabby town go to the loo right in front of you. It's hard to take them seriously when you've seen them poo. There's a reason Cleopatra, Queen of Egypt, greets her people from a perfumed barge rather than straining away on a public lav.

Leader of Egypt

Leader of Pompeii

June XXVI

I was passing the town's bakery today when I felt a blast of heat from one of its ovens. I glanced inside the bakery and saw a donkey turning a mill.

OF COURSE! This was the answer to Numerius's second clue.

Go from cold to hot, where the blind beast circles.

Bakers use a donkey to turn the mill and grind the corn. And they cover its eyes so it doesn't get too distracted. So the bakery is the hot place Numerius meant, and the donkey is the circling blind beast. GENIUS!

I rushed inside to try and find the next
clue, but one of the bakers accused me of
trying to steal bread and chased me out
with a knife. I was about to reason with him
when I noticed some red graffiti scrawled
around the doorway. Most of it was just
the usual nonsense, like 'Figulus loves Idaia'

or 'This bread tastes like stone', but there was a small line scrawled just above the door.

YOUR SEARCH ENDS UNDER THE ROWS OF RELAXATION AND RELIEF.

This must be the final clue. At last I'm nearing the end of the trail Numerius laid down. The only problem is, I have NO idea at all what it means.

June XXVIII

I wandered around town today thinking about the clue. But when the answer finally came to me, I wished it hadn't.

I was approaching the forum when a horrible smell wafted into my nostrils. At once, I could see this was the place Numerius meant. The public toilets. What are toilets except rows where people go for relaxation and relief? And if my search was leading to the place UNDER them, I was going to have to climb INSIDE the sewer.

I considered giving up. If Numerius had set a trail of clues that led to the inside of a toilet, he was obviously crazy. Who knows what he wanted me to discover? Maybe he was secretly living down there.

But then I thought ... what if he'd hidden something REALLY secret down there, something he wanted only the most dedicated person – a true Roman hero – to find? Wouldn't it be the ideal place?

I had to investigate. One of the rows of seats had a hole smashed in the side, so I squeezed myself through and splashed down into the stream of water underneath.

I found myself slipping on the squishy floor and had to steady myself on the slimy walls. The smell was so strong it made my eyes water, but I managed to hold my breath and look around. The holes above threw dim light on the narrow space. I tramped under each row of toilets, desperate to find a hidden object. But there was nothing except for a disgusting swamp of poo and wee.

So this was it. Numerius WAS crazy after all. I'd followed the trail of a madman and ended up inside a public toilet.

And that's when I did what I'd promised myself I wouldn't do. I began to wonder how things could possibly get worse.

I heard feet stomping into the toilet above me. Loud voices were yakking about the mountain demon. Then, one by one, the circles of light above me disappeared.

I won't go into too much detail about what happened next, as I've spent the rest of today trying to force it out of my mind. I can only say that it was like being caught in a fart thunderstorm.

I couldn't even beg them to stop. They would have thought I was a toilet demon.

I can't write about my ordeal, but when it was over, I crawled out again and dashed into the baths. I threw myself into the cold pool and dunked myself under the water until I was finally clean.

Pontius and Spurius passed by again. Spurius pointed at me and said, 'Dirtius Maximus. Roman weirdo.'

For once, I had to agree with him.

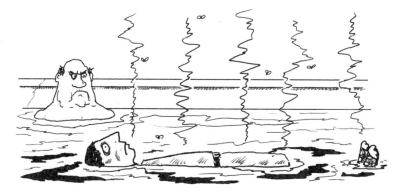

June XXIX

Dad has given up trying to talk sense into Pontius and Pullo, which is understandable. He's arranging a meeting in the forum so he can address all the people of Pompeii directly. He thinks they'll listen to reason and agree to pay the extra tax.

I don't have high hopes. The people of Pompeii are about as capable of listening to reason as Mum's chickens.

I'll just have to hope he's right, though. It's my only chance of escape from this ridiculous stinky place.

July 1

I was passing the theatre this morning when something occurred to me. The 'rows of relaxation and relief" could refer to the theatre, not the toilets. After all, people go there to relax, and they feel great relief at the end of a tense tragedy.

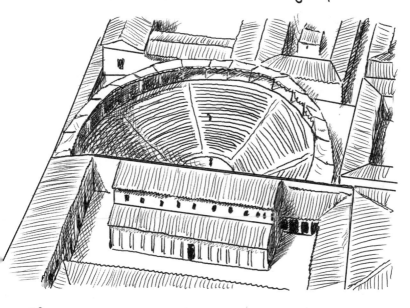

My heart lifted – I might have solved the final clue. Then it sank again as I remembered I'd made myself endure the fart storm inside the toilets for nothing.

I rushed inside the theatre and looked at the rows of stone seats. I couldn't see anywhere to hide things.

I got on to my hands and knees and crawled along the bottom row. There was a loose stone halfway along it. This was it! I'd finally reached the end of the secret trail!

'What are you doing?'

I looked over my shoulder. A girl was peering down at me. I couldn't believe I'd got so distracted I'd forgotten to keep a watch out for snoopers.

'I'm rehearsing for a play,' I said.

'Why are you on your hands and knees?' asked the girl.

'Er ... I'm playing a dog,' I said. 'Now if you don't mind, I need to prepare. Bow wow wow!'

I hoped my barking would make the girl go away, but she just stood there.

'Bow wow wow,' I tried again.

'That's fine,' she said. 'I just thought you might have come here because of Numerius.'

'Bow wow ... oh,' I said and got to my feet.

'Er, no,' said the girl. 'You didn't think the rows of relaxation and relief were the public toilets, did you?'

'No,' I said. 'Of course not. I just thought you might have done. Anyway, never mind about that. I think I've found something.'

I crouched down and pulled the stone out. There was a hollow gap behind and a scroll inside.

'Brilliant!' said the girl, as I grabbed the scroll and unravelled it.

FROJUDWXODWLRQV RQ ILQGLQJ
WKLV VFUROO. EHIRUH L IOHG L
SURPLVHG L ZRXOG QHYHU WHOO
DQBRQH ZKDW L KDG GLVFRYHUHG.
EXW LI BRX DUH FOHYHU HQRXJK WR
EH UHDGLQJ WKLV BRX GHVHUYH
WR NQRZ.

WKURXJK PB VWXGLHV L KDYH
GLVFRYHUHG WKDW WKH UHFHQW
WUHPRUV KDYH EHHQ FDXVHG EB
DLU PRYLQJ XQGHU WKH HDUWK.
HYHQWXDOOB WKLV ZLOO FDXVH

74

WKH PRXQWDLQ WR HASORGH.
GHDGOB JDV ZLOO OHDN RXW,
EXUQLQJ URFNV ZLOO IDOO DQG
OLTXLG ILUH ZLOO IORZ.

BHW ZKHQ L VKDUHG PB GLVFRYHULHV
ZLWK SRQWLXV DQG SXOOR WKHB
LQVLVWHG LW ZDV DOO FDXVHG EB
D GHPRQ DQG WKUHDWHQHG PH LI L
VSUHDG PB OLHV.

EXW BRX DUH VPDUW HQRXJK WR
KDYH IROORZHG WKH WUDLO DQG
FUDFNHG WKH FRGH VR L DP VXUH
BRX ZLOO KHHG PB ZDUQLQJ.

OHDYH SRPSHLL ZKLOH BRX
VWLOO FDQ.

I think the man in the picture was Julius Caesar, because I recognized his silly hairstyle. But I have no idea what the writing was supposed to mean. All that fuss for a load of gibberish. Maybe Numerius was mad after all.

July II

The girl's name is Decima. She's also just moved here from Rome. Turns out, like me, she went to Numerius's house to look for scrolls and got drawn into the trail of clues. Unlike me, she didn't have to suffer a poo thunderstorm on the way.

Decima's dad owns some shops in Rome, and he's brought loads of stuff to Pompeii to trade for fish sauce. I'm sure he'll change his mind when he tastes the stuff, but in the meantime it will be good to have Decima, a fellow Roman, around.

I went to her house today and we had another look at the weird message on the scroll. I didn't get any further with it, but I told Decima I'd met Julius Caesar and he thought I was a BRILLIANT Roman hero. She seemed quite impressed.

July III

About two hundred people came to Dad's meeting in the forum this afternoon. It wasn't a bad turnout, especially as he admitted he was going to talk about boring tax matters.

His speech was very clear, but I could tell it was going over the heads of the locals.

Blank expressions

The people of Pompeii

When Dad finished, he asked the crowd if they had any questions.

'Yeah,' said a man at the back in a blue tunic. 'What are you going to do about the demon on Mount Vesuvius?'

'I meant tax questions,' said Dad.

'Will the demon stay away if we make more animal sacrifices?' asked a woman with red hair. 'I heard it has two heads.'

'That's enough!' shouted Dad. 'If I hear one more word about this stupid demon ...'

Suddenly, the ground rumbled, jolting everything from side to side. A cart loaded with jars of fish sauce overturned and spilled its stinky contents. A chunk of stone crashed down from the roof of the temple, and Dad had to leap out of the way.

'It's the demon!' shouted the woman with red hair. 'You've angered it. It heard you calling it stupid.'

The crowd scattered and I wandered over to Dad, who slumped down on the steps.

'I told you they were an odd bunch,' I said. 'Never mind. We'll be home soon.'

Dad looked down at his scroll and sighed.

'No, we won't,' said Dad. 'Julius Caesar said I can't return until they've agreed to pay the extra tax.'

'WHAT?' I shouted. 'You said we were just here for the summer.'

'That's how long I thought it would take,' he said. 'Still, at least your mother's happy. She'd stay here forever, given the chance.'

Never mind her. What about me? I can't stay here forever. I'm destined to be a great Roman hero, not a fish sauce seller in some irrelevant little backwater. BAH!

July IV

This morning I told Decima about Dad's meeting. Like everyone else, she was more interested in the mountain demon than the tax reforms. Unlike the others, she thought that the idea there is a monster was a load of superstitious nonsense.

She reckons we should go up the mountain to find out what's really causing the rumbles.

I agreed, although I was only really agreeing that it was the SORT of thing we could do. I wasn't committing myself to her plan.

I suggested we spend some more time trying to work out what the scroll says instead. But then Decima accused me of being frightened of the imaginary demon, which obviously I'm not.

So we're meeting at first light tomorrow to go up the mountain and investigate.

UPDATE
Okay, I admit it. I AM a bit scared. I know it's really, really, really unlikely there's a demon up there. But what if there is? I'm going to see if Dad brought any weapons with him.

UPDATE
He didn't bring any, but I found some useful stuff to take.

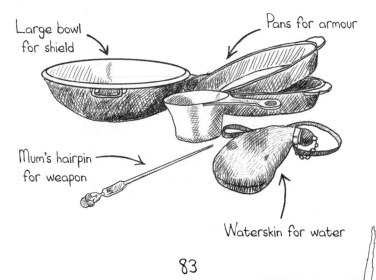

Large bowl for shield

Pans for armour

Mum's hairpin for weapon

Waterskin for water

Put it all together and what do you get?

GUARANTEED DEMON-PROOFING

UPDATE

I practised my demon-busting moves in the atrium tonight. I jabbed forward with the hairpin and swung the bowl round over and over again for protection. I think I got a little carried away, because I kept imagining there was a real demon lashing out at me and shooting fire from its nostrils. I leapt back so quickly from this pretend fire that I knocked one of Mum's pottery vases to the floor and smashed it.

What I imagined
I was doing

What I
actually did

My cheeks flushed. The vase was
TOTALLY shattered and would be
impossible to mend. AND I'd knocked it down
from a high shelf, so I wouldn't be able to
blame it on the chickens.

I was still stressing about the vase when
another massive rumble shook the house.
I heard shrill screams and clattering in the
street outside.

Mum came rushing in. 'My vase!' she screamed. 'The stomping of the mountain demon has destroyed it.'

'Er ... yes,' I said. 'That's exactly what just happened. Demons, eh? What can you do?'

If I do run into this demon tomorrow I should probably thank it rather than fight it. It's just saved me from a MASSIVE telling off.

July V

Decima giggled when she saw me this morning. That's hardly an appropriate reaction to a true Roman hero.

'What are you wearing?' she asked.

'Demon-proofing,' I said. 'Just in case.'

'What are you going to do?' she asked. 'Attack it or cook it a delicious stew?'

We left town by the Salt Gate and headed towards the mountain. As the sun rose, I felt sweat trickling down my tunic. It was so hot with my pans on, but I thought about all the armour Roman soldiers have to wear. If they can do it, so could I.

My mouth felt as dry as the dust under my sandals and I was glad I had the water.

'Can I have some?' asked Decima.

'Maybe being prepared isn't such a bad idea after all,' I said, handing her the leather pouch. 'Who looks silly now?'

'Still you,' she said. 'But thanks for the water.'

We passed through an olive grove and into a sloping vineyard.

'Did you hear that?' asked Decima.

'What?' I really couldn't hear much above the clatter of my pans.

'It might help if you kept still, Kitchen Implement Boy,' she said.

I froze. There was a low growl coming from the row of vines to my left. I saw a black shape flitting among the green plants.

'It's the demon!' I shouted. My hands were shaking so hard it was difficult to keep hold of my bowl shield.

'Excellent,' said Decima, striding ahead. 'Let's take a look at it.'

I tried to follow Decima. I really did. I told my body to move forwards, but instead I found myself throwing the shield and hairpin to the ground and running down the slope.

The growls of the demon were getting louder. I could hear the beast's feet thundering behind me. There seemed to be a lot of feet. Was this some sort of huge spider demon?

I turned to look, but sweat poured down from my pan helmet into my eyes and I could only make out a vague two-headed shape.

I faced forwards again, but was too late to see a huge rock. I tripped over it and tumbled to the ground. Small, gritty stones broke the skin on my arms and bright pain jolted into my ankle.

I could hear the demon's deep growl getting closer. This was it. I was at the mercy of a massive mountain monster.

July VI

I should explain. I wasn't really attacked by a demon yesterday. It was just a couple of black dogs that live in the vineyard. And they didn't really attack me. They just yapped a bit and licked my face.

What really happened

I twisted my ankle when I fell, and Decima had to help me back to town. It took us ages to get down the mountain.

Mum came to my room last night looking for her hairpin, and gasped when she saw my cuts and bruises. She asked what had happened and I was about to tell the truth, but then I realized I'd have to admit to stealing the hairpin.

'I was attacked by the demon,' I said.

I know I shouldn't have lied, but it was all I could think of. I hope the gods don't punish me for it.

They haven't done so far, though.

July VII

I wanted to stay in bed this morning, but Mum insisted I come out and tell her friends about my demon encounter. Pontius, Pullo and loads of other townspeople were rammed into the atrium waiting to hear from me.

I wanted to admit that I had made the whole thing up, but I think my public-speaking skills must have taken over ... I gave an exciting account of how the demon leapt on me and pinned me to the ground with its sharp talons. I explained it had two heads, rows of gleaming teeth and eyes that glowed with orange fire.

I described how I'd wrestled it away, kicked its furry bottom and sent it howling back up the mountain.

Some of Mum's friends started wailing
and throwing their hands up in the air, and
I wondered if I'd made my speech a little
TOO GOOD.

'We mustn't panic!' shouted Pontius.

'Let's step up our animal sacrifices,' said Pullo. 'Tell everyone to bring animals to the temple for immediate slaughter.'

They rushed out. I really should have called them back in and admitted I had made it all up. I see that now.

'I heard all that,' shouted Dad from his study. 'Dorkius, don't tell me you've started believing all that demon nonsense, too.'

'No,' I said. 'It's all part of my plan to get them to agree to pay the extra tax.'

This wasn't strictly true, but I'll probably come up with a plan at some point, and I'll pretend this was part of it.

July VIII

I couldn't go anywhere today without people asking about the demon attack. I must have told the story FIFTY times. In the end, I was adding in bits about how I chopped off one of the demon's heads only to see it grow back and sneer at me. It's nice to be appreciated in this town for something, even if it is for making up far-fetched lies.

July IX

My speech about the demon has clearly had a BIG impact on Mum's friends. This morning I heard Pullo talking to her about it.

'The demon will attack soon,' he was saying. 'All the signs point to it.'

'What signs?' asked Mum.

'Strange patterns of lightning have been observed,' said Pullo. 'Birds have been seen flying in unusual formations, and one of my cows gave birth to a piglet.'

'Oh no!' wailed Mum. 'What terrible omens.'

'Actually, it might have been one of the sows who gave birth to the piglet,' said Pullo. 'It was hard to see in the dark.'

July X

I came back to my room this afternoon to find a man painting a scary face on the wall.

'What is that?' I asked.

The painter stopped and looked at me. 'A Medusa. That's what your mum ordered.'

'Why would she do that?' I asked.

'It's in case that demon comes,' he said.
'The best way to protect against evil things
is to draw something even more terrifying
to frighten them off. Everyone knows that.'

'Oh,' I said. I was going to ask if he could
make the picture slightly less scary so I could
sleep at night, but I thought it wouldn't
make me sound very heroic.

The painter finished the hideous image and
took a step back.

'There you go,' he said. 'That should keep the
pesky thing away.'

'Er ... thanks,' I said. 'I think.'

'No. Thank you,' he said. 'I've been doing

a roaring trade since you told everyone about the demon. Tell you what, I'll add a screaming face with blood pouring from the eyes for free. My way of saying thanks.'

'No, I'm sure this will do the trick,' I said.

Now I've got to try and get to sleep with the monstrous face staring down at me. This isn't going to be easy.

GULP!

July XI

Decima came round this morning. She looked pretty annoyed, so I pretended to be asleep, but it didn't make any difference.

'Why did you tell everyone you saw a two-headed demon?' she asked. She was carrying the scroll we'd found in the theatre and I was worried she was going to hit me with it.

'So Mum wouldn't be angry I stole her hairpin,' I said.

'You sent the ENTIRE town into a frenzy of panic just for that?' she asked.

It did sound quite bad when she put it like that. 'Yeah. Sorry.'

'You can make it up to me by working out what this code means,' she said, throwing the strange scroll we'd found at me. 'I'm convinced Numerius leaving town and the weird rumbles in the ground are related. And this scroll can tell us why. But my head hurts from trying to work it out. It's your turn now, Dorkius.'

July XII

I feel terrible about making all that stuff up and upsetting Decima, and I really want to make it up to her by working out what the message on the scroll means. But it STILL looks like complete nonsense.

Okay, let me think about this ... There's a picture of Caesar above a load of random letters. Caesar must be the important clue. So what do I know about him?

Silly hairstyle

Unconvincing distraction

1. He has a silly hairstyle, and he tries to distract everyone from it by wearing a laurel wreath.

11. His hobbies include fighting, public speaking and riding in AWESOME military parades.

III. He's a noble Roman hero, except when Queen Cleopatra of Egypt is around. Then he becomes soppy and embarrassing.

Hmmmm. None of this is really helping. He certainly spouts a lot of gibberish when he's with Cleopatra, but it's usually stuff about love and romance rather than a random collection of letters.

What's the connection between our (sometimes) great leader and the secret message? This is going to drive me MAD.

July XIII

BRILLIANT news. I've cracked the code!

I was chatting to Dad about Caesar, to see if he mentioned anything that might help me. Dad went on about all the battles Caesar fought. I was just beginning to drift off when he mentioned that Caesar invented something called a 'cipher'. Caesar's cipher let him send secret messages during battles.

It's quite simple, really. All you have to do is shift everything three letters down the alphabet, so that 'D' means 'A', 'E' means 'B' and 'F' means 'C' etc. If you apply this to the words on the scroll, you get:

CONGRATULATIONS ON FINDING THIS
SCROLL. BEFORE I FLED I PROMISED
I WOULD NEVER TELL ANYONE WHAT
I HAD DISCOVERED. BUT IF YOU ARE
CLEVER ENOUGH TO BE READING THIS
YOU DESERVE TO KNOW.

THROUGH MY STUDIES I HAVE
DISCOVERED THAT THE RECENT
TREMORS HAVE BEEN CAUSED BY
AIR MOVING UNDER THE EARTH.
EVENTUALLY THIS WILL CAUSE THE
MOUNTAIN TO EXPLODE. DEADLY GAS

WILL LEAK OUT, BURNING ROCKS WILL FALL AND LIQUID FIRE WILL FLOW.

YET WHEN I SHARED MY DISCOVERIES WITH PONTIUS AND PULLO THEY INSISTED IT WAS ALL CAUSED BY A DEMON AND THREATENED ME IF I SPREAD MY LIES.

BUT YOU ARE SMART ENOUGH TO HAVE FOLLOWED THE TRAIL AND CRACKED THE CODE SO I AM SURE YOU WILL HEED MY WARNING.

LEAVE POMPEII WHILE YOU STILL CAN.

July XIV

Decima was impressed when I showed her how I'd cracked the code. We were both so pleased, it took a while for the scroll's grim message to sink in.

This town is going to get swamped with something even more toxic than fish sauce. Burning rocks are going to rain down and, knowing my luck, they'll all land right on my head. It's not really something to celebrate.

UPDATE
Oh gods! I just looked back at the first entry in my scroll and saw the words of Mum's old soothsayer.

It looks as though he was right for once. We need to get out of Pompeii NOW!

A mighty roar will split the earth. Fire will flow and rocks will fall. Slaves, freedmen and citizens will be buried side by side.

July XV

I just went into Dad's office and told him about the secret scroll, but he didn't seem to care.

'If it's not two-headed demons with you, it's exploding mountains,' he said.

'I'm sorry I made up that stuff about the demon,' I said. 'But this is REAL. Burning rocks are going to rain down on us. We need to leave.'

'You might be right,' said Dad. 'But burning rocks will seem like a Saturnalia present compared to what Julius Caesar will do to me if I return without getting the tax changes agreed.'

Angry Vesuvius

Angry Caesar

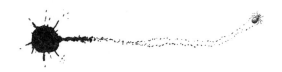

July XVI

Decima's dad has also refused to leave town. He said she's been reading too many scrolls and it has sent her imagination into overdrive.

So instead Decima's come up with a plan to get us out of here. I think it might work, but I'm not looking forward to it.

Pontius and Pullo have called a town meeting tomorrow to discuss the demon. Decima wants me to pretend that I've remembered something really important about my demon encounter. Then, when I've got the crowd's attention, I can tell them the truth about what Numerius said in his scroll.

I know my public-speaking skills are good, but in the scroll, Numerius says Pontius and Pullo threatened him when he tried to warn them about the mountain and trapped air. What will they do to me if I make them angry?

Decima ran out before I could come up with a different plan that didn't involve me infuriating the whole town and getting pelted with rotten vegetables.

At least it's better than burning rocks.

July XVII

The crowd didn't pelt me with rotten vegetables. It was much worse than that.

I climbed up the temple steps and looked out at them. There were LOADS more people than at the tax discussion.

'I know you want to hear about my demon attack,' I said. 'But I'm not going to talk about it.'

A loud 'BOO' rang out. I spotted a man in a blue tunic at the back wandering away.

'But what I have to tell you is even more exciting,' I said.

'What is it?' asked a woman with red hair.

'Have you been attacked by a manticore this time? Or a basilisk? They're good.'

The man in the blue tunic turned back to join the crowd again. 'Was it a gorgon?' he asked. 'My sister's friend got bitten by one of those once. Nasty!'

Manticore

Basilisk

Gorgon

'Nothing like that,' I said. 'The truth is, there is no demon or any other type of beast in the mountain. It's Vesuvius ITSELF that's the problem. I know because I found a secret scroll left by Numerius.'

'Not that nutter Numerius,' shouted Pullo. 'I might have known he'd leave some sort of message for weirdos to find.'

'There's air trapped underneath the mountain,' I shouted. 'And it's going to EXPLODE, sending rocks and fire all over the place and all over us.'

I'd expected everyone to flee in panic at this point, but they just kept staring at me.

'Abandon the town!' I shouted. 'It's not safe.'

There was another awkward pause.

'I think the demon must have taken over his mind,' said Pontius. 'That's why he's spouting gibberish.'

The crowd wailed. 'Save him!' shouted Mum. 'Somebody save my poor Dorky Worky.'

Hearing Mum call me 'Dorky Worky' in front of everyone made me blush bright red.

'Look! The heat of the demon is showing on his face,' shouted Pullo. 'We must act fast. Someone fetch some fish sauce. That's great for curing things.'

Pontius rushed up the steps and twisted my hands behind my back. A stall owner followed him, clutching a jar of the rancid fish sauce.

'Please stop!' I begged.

The stall owner poured the sauce into my mouth. I tried to tell him I was feeling better, but he kept on going for AGES. I could feel the puke rising inside me. I tried to hold it in, but it was no use. I spewed everywhere.

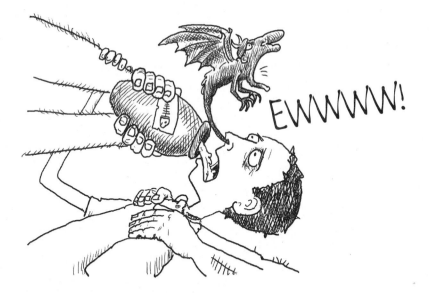

EWWWW!

'I think the demon's gone now,' said Pontius.

'Let's not panic,' shouted Pullo. 'As long as we keep sacrificing animals, the gods will come to our aid. Tell everyone to bring more animals to the temple immediately.'

July XVIII

The whole town smells really nasty today. Obviously, the town always smells nasty, but today it was more like fart than fish sauce. I wondered if there'd been an outbreak of food poisoning.

Across the street from our house a woman was shouting, 'Who has killed my poor fish?'

A man ran up to her with a handful of dead sparrows. 'That's nothing. These just fell on to my head from a tree. Know anyone who might want to buy them?'

I wonder if it was something to do with the smell. Is it possible to do a fart so stinky it actually kills things? My friend Cornelius once did one so terrible he got a whole row to himself in the amphitheatre. But I'm pretty sure even THAT didn't kill anything. Whoever did it could make a fortune performing at beast shows. I'd definitely pay to see a lion being farted to death.

PARP!

July XIX

The air is still thick with fart smell. Everyone in town is talking about it. I spotted Pontius and Pullo discussing it with the rest of the local government outside a tavern.

'The mountain demon has mocked our animal sacrifices by farting all our birds and fish to death,' said Pullo.

'Excellent,' said Pontius. 'That proves we're annoying it. We need to make sure we keep it up. Let's sacrifice an animal every hour until the gods chase the demon away.'

'That might be a problem,' said Pullo. 'The gods don't seem very interested in saving us, and we're running out of animals.'

The gods, NOT helping the people of Pompeii anytime soon.

'Never mind,' said Pontius. 'We can simply dip into our emergency funds and buy some animals from our neighbours in Herculaneum.'

Emergency funds? That proves they could pay the extra tax RIGHT NOW if they wanted. Then I could be back in lovely Rome rather than wasting my time in this guffy little backwater.

July XX

I saw Pullo leading a white bull towards the temple this morning. I'd hate to think how much he'd forked out for it. If he keeps wasting the emergency funds on animals, he won't be able to pay the extra tax even if he wants to.

Everyone was crowding round to look at the poor creature as it walked through the forum.

Pontius was waiting between two of the columns at the top of the steps. 'Excellent choice,' he said. 'That should do the trick.'

A rumble shook the ground and some red roof tiles from the nearby houses smashed at his feet.

'Quick!' shouted Pontius. 'Sacrifice the bull before the demon can mock us further.'

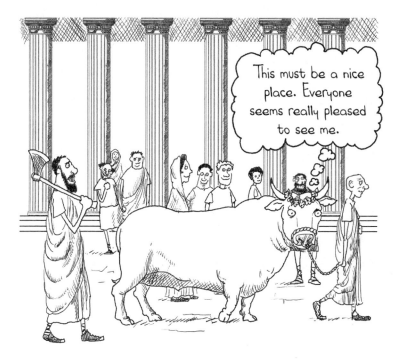

July XXI

I'm convinced these rumbles and horrible smells are a sign the mountain is about to explode. Numerius mentioned 'deadly gas' just before 'burning rocks' and 'liquid fire'. That means it's going to happen SOON.

I tried really hard to get Mum to leave today, but it was no use.

'That mountain is going to explode,' I said. 'We will all perish.'

'You mustn't worry, Dorkius,' said Mum. 'Pontius and Pullo are doing plenty of animal sacrifices, so I'm sure everything will be fine.'

'They're not going to change anything,' I said. 'The air trapped in the mountain is going to make it blow up and it doesn't matter how many white bulls those fools waste money on. I'm going to get out of this dangerous town whether you come with me or not.'

'Why don't you have a nice relaxing lie down?' asked Mum.

'Because Pompeii is a death trap,' I said. 'I could no more have a nice relaxing lie down here than in the middle of an amphitheatre full of angry, starving lions.'

Sometimes if you stop worrying about your problems, they simply go away.

July XXII

I noticed a large man with a red face striding over to Pontius and Pullo in the forum today. Spurius stood up. 'This is Pompous Fatso, magistrate of Herculaneum.'

Pontius smiled and waved. The large man's face went even redder. 'My name is Pomponious Falto. If my nomenclator were as bad as yours, I'd whip him in the forum.'

'What can we do for you?' asked Pullo.

'You can stop buying all the animals from my town and sacrificing them,' said Pomponious. 'Everything is grinding to a halt without work animals. The wagon drivers can't deliver, the farmers can't plough their land and the bakers can't make bread.'

'We didn't force anyone to sell their animals and we paid a good price,' said Pontius.

'Those short-sighted fools can't resist your money,' said Pomponious. 'So I'm telling you to stop or those animals won't be the only ones in danger.'

There! ANOTHER reason to get out of town. Even if the mountain doesn't explode, there'll be a war with Herculaneum.

The rampaging, murderous hordes of Herculaneum.

July XXIII

I spotted that painter outside our house again today. He was drawing a rude picture of some private parts right next to our door.

'Stop that at once!' I shouted. 'Or I'll tell Pontius and Pullo about it.'

'Pontius and Pullo?' he asked. 'They were the ones who ordered it. I'm painting this picture on every house to protect against the demon. It's a very powerful good luck symbol, you know.'

I felt my cheeks flushing, so I dashed back inside, so he wouldn't think the demon was heating up my face again.

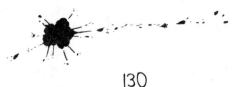

July XXIV

When I came home this afternoon I heard
a strange oinking noise coming from my room.
I rushed inside and saw two pigs lurking in
the corner. I asked Mum what was going on
and she said Pontius and Pullo had bought

too many animals to fit into the temple, so they're asking people to look after the extras until they're slaughtered. I hope they hurry up and get through the backlog, or my precious sleep is going to be sacrificed too.

OINK!
OINK!

July XXV

Decima's dad told me she wasn't in when I went round today, but I spotted her peeping out of her window.

'Stand with your back to the wall,' hissed Decima. 'Don't make it look like you're talking to me, in case Dad finds out.'

I leant against the wall and stared down at the street. 'What's happened?'

'Dad's banished me to my room because I kept telling him we had to leave Pompeii,' said Decima.

'My parents are sick of me telling them too,' I said.

'We need to get out of here, Dorkius,' said Decima. 'If our parents won't leave, we'll just have to run away on our own. Come back here after everyone has gone to sleep tonight and we can escape before the mountain explodes. I'll borrow some of Dad's supplies so we can set up a camp.'

'Alright,' I said. 'It seems like we've got no choice.'

I glanced up the street and saw Pontius and Spurius approaching.

'This is Doltus Maximus,' said Spurius. 'He's talking to himself because he's a Roman weirdo.'

'I know who this fool is,' said Pontius, glaring at me. 'He's been spreading silly lies he got from that nerd Numerius. If it weren't for his lovely mother, I'd expel him from town.'

I wish he WOULD expel me. Escaping back to Rome is EXACTLY what I want. As punishments go, it would be right up there with a delicious eight-course meal.

July XXVI

It wasn't hard for me to stay awake with those pigs oinking.

When I was sure everyone was asleep, I sneaked out and made my way to Decima's house. I considered waking my parents up and making one last effort to convince them to come, but I knew it would be no use. I'll just have to hope they escape in time if the mountain starts spewing fire.

Decima was waiting in the atrium and she showed me into her dad's supply room.

We found some brilliant wooden carrying frames that are used by soldiers. I also found two wolf headdresses and I wanted to take them because they looked cool, but Decima said they'd make us too hot.

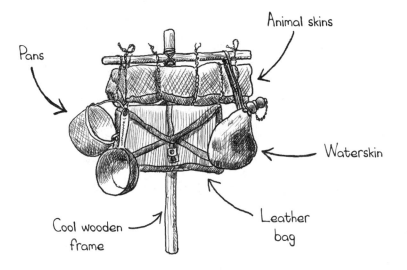

Animal skins

Pans

Waterskin

Cool wooden frame

Leather bag

'Who's there?' shouted Decima's dad from his bedroom. 'Is someone in my supply room?'

'Quick!' whispered Decima. We ran out of the house and off down the dark street. I could hear Decima's dad shouting 'thieving Pompeian dogs' from inside the house.

As we passed through the forum, Decima pointed to one of the columns opposite the temple. The donkey from the bakery was tied to it.

'Pontius must be planning to sacrifice it tomorrow,' said Decima. 'Let's take it for our escape.'

'Good idea!' I whispered. 'I'm brilliant at riding horses, so I expect I'll be great at riding donkeys, too.'

I ran over to the donkey and untied its ropes. I clambered onto its back and helped Decima up.

'Forward!' I hissed.

The donkey trundled ahead, but veered to the right. It trotted in a circle, ending up where it had started.

'Come on!' I hissed. 'Straight ahead.'

The donkey circled again.

And again.

'Not such a brilliant idea after all,' I said. So we got down and continued on foot.

We ran through the Forum Gate and headed inland, trying to get as far away from Vesuvius as we could.

Decima insisted we keep marching all day, even though the wooden frame was digging into my shoulder and I really wanted a break.

We were miles away from Vesuvius by the time Decima found a spot she was happy with. Burning rocks will never reach us here.

We set up a tent using the animal skins and some branches. Then we crawled inside. I tried to entertain Decima by practising my public-speaking skills, but I soon heard her snoring. I knew she'd tire herself out with all that walking.

July XXVII

No sign of any explosions yet.

A cloud

July XXVIII

Still nothing.

A tree

July XXIX

Nope. Nothing.

Some rocks

July XXX

THERE WAS A MASSIVE EXPLOSION TODAY ...

Only joking. NOTHING happened.

July XXXI

Still nothing today. Maybe Numerius WAS mad after all.

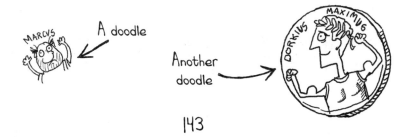

MARCVS

A doodle

Another doodle

DORKIVS MAXIMVS

August I

Our food supplies are running low and Decima's feeling guilty about running away and leaving her parents to perish. She wants to go back to Pompeii tomorrow. Maybe we panicked too much about the mountain. Even if Numerius was right, it doesn't mean it's going to blow up right now. It could happen in a hundred years' time.

August II

I can hardly BELIEVE what happened today. I'm still shaking ...

We packed up our tent at first light and set off. The sun was boiling and I struggled to keep up with Decima who strode on ahead. My pack was weighing me down so much I was staggering from side to side.

'Wait!' I shouted. 'Let's find some shade to rest in.' But Decima ignored me. Eventually I threw my pack to the ground and collapsed on top of it.

'Sorry,' said Decima, rushing back to me. 'We can take a break now if you like.'

I was too weak to speak. I nodded and closed my eyes.

When I opened my eyes, the sun was low. I realized I must have slept right through until evening. But it didn't feel like evening. It was still boiling hot.

I squinted at Decima. Her eyes were wide and her mouth was hanging open.

I turned to see what she was looking at. A jet of orange flame was leaping into the sky from the summit of the mountain. Above it, smoke was spreading through the air in the shape of massive mushroom.

That fart smell was back, too, but now it was mixed with a bitter burning aroma that was so strong I could taste it in my mouth.

Swirling grey soot blew into my eyes and stung them. I looked down at my tunic and saw it was covered in splodges of dirt. I wiped one and it left a thick grey stain.

'Mum's not going to be happy about that,' I said. 'She hates it when I get my tunic dirty.'

'I think your mum will have bigger things to worry about back in Pompeii,' said Decima.

'Oh yeah,' I said, trying not to think about what might be happening to my parents. Pompeii was much closer to the mountain than we were. Decima looked really worried.

'As long as we don't panic, we'll be fine,' I reassured her. 'Ow! What was that?' Something had whacked into my forehead.

Decima pointed to a small, black rock at my feet. I tried to pick it up, but it was too hot. Another rock whizzed past my ear.

'I've changed my mind. PANIC!' I shouted, and we grabbed our packs and began to run away from the mountain.

Huge flakes of grey dirt swirled through the air. I looked over my shoulder and saw plumes of thick smoke billowing towards us. More rocks thudded on to the ground.

My heart hammered in my chest and I found myself running faster. Decima was just a few paces ahead, but it was difficult to see her through the blizzard of grey flakes.

'Watch!' I shouted.

I untied the saucepan from my pack and put it on my head. A tiny rock bounced off the pan. Decima did the same.

Then something very strange happened.
The image of a baby appeared in the thick
grey smoke ahead of me. I wondered if the
fumes had driven me mad.

The baby turned into a toddler and then a
young child ...

I couldn't believe it. My life was flashing
before my eyes ...

... and my brain was choosing all the least heroic bits!

What about the day I saved Caesar in a BRILLIANT sword fight? Or the day I took part in a SPECTACULAR military parade?

I was determind to show my stupid memory I was a hero after all by outrunning the rocks and smoke. So I charged forward at full speed ... that is until I tripped over a rock and fell flat on my face, ramming the handle of the pan into the ground.

By the time I'd managed to unjam the pan handle, the smoke had cleared and the fart smell had faded.

'I think the wind's blowing it the other way,' said Decima. 'It must be awful back in Pompeii. They're so close to the mountain.'

I wondered if Pontius and Pullo were still trying to find more animals to sacrifice. They must be getting pretty desperate.

Soon the wind had blown the smoke further away, revealing the top of the mountain.

I gasped and leapt to my feet. Fire was flowing down it in a bright orange river. It was seeping over the plains at amazing speed and heading RIGHT FOR US.

RUN!

Decima pointed to a steep hill rising from the plain to our right. 'Let's head there. If we can get halfway up, we might be alright.'

I darted towards the hill as the heat from the approaching fire seared my skin.

After a couple of minutes, I glanced over my shoulder. I couldn't see Decima. In fact, the flowing orange fire was so bright I could hardly see anything at all.

I squinted at a crumpled heap a hundred paces back. Decima! She was trying to get to her feet, but kept collapsing.

The fire was almost upon her. My instinct was to keep going up the hill. If I tried to go back and help Decima, we'd both be engulfed by it. We'd never get back home and I would never grow up to be a noble Roman hero.

I was about to keep going when I remembered how Decima had helped me when I'd fallen over on the mountain. How could I abandon her after that? More to the point, how could I ever grow up to be a noble Roman hero if I left my friend to be swamped by liquid fire?

I had to try and help her. Even if we both ended up getting frazzled. I ran to her.

'Go back!' shouted Decima. 'Leave me or we'll both die.'

'A noble hero never leaves his friends,' I shouted. Or at least, I tried to shout it. The heat dried my throat out, and hardly any sound came out.

I put my arm around Decima's shoulder and hoisted her up. She tried stepping on to her left foot, but yelped with pain.

'I think I've busted that ankle,' she yelled.

I dragged her and she hopped as fast as she could, but it was no use. We were moving slower than a Pompeian gladiator.

'Come on!' I shouted. 'We can do this.'

We reached the base of the hill. Decima was throwing all her weight into every hop, almost pulling both of us over each time.

The fire was nearly upon us. The reek of the mountain fart was back and it was so strong I felt like fainting. It smelt even worse than when I was trapped underneath the toilets.

We kept on hobbling and hopping up the hill. I steered us around rocks and bushes, knowing that any slip would send us tumbling down into the bubbling fire.

The hill grew steeper and every hop became harder. The fart fumes must have confused my brain because I started to think I was a dormouse being cooked by our chef.

'Look!' shouted Decima and pointed. Below us the fire was beginning to flow around the base of the hill and not up it. We'd escaped it.

August III

We're still on the hillside. The orange liquid has flown away, leaving a trail of fires all along the plain.

What are we going to do now? We can't go back to Pompeii. It must surely have been destroyed. I can only hope that Mum and Dad escaped.

UPDATE
The sun has risen. I just climbed to the top of the hill and saw Pompeii to the south-east of the mountain. I thought it would be buried in grey dust, but it actually looks pretty normal. It's just a tiny spot in the distance, so it's hard to tell, but I couldn't see any smoke rising from it.

Pompeii

I told Decima, and she wants to go back immediately. I agreed, but told her to prepare for the worst. We could be about to walk into the world's biggest tomb.

UPDATE
We're a few miles away from Pompeii now and it's getting dark again. I wanted to wait until tomorrow to go back into Pompeii, but Decima is determined to go now in case there are any injured people we can help.

I'm worried we might see some ghosts in there, but I've come up with a BRILLIANT way of repelling them. I remembered what the painter said about scaring off evil things, so I scratched a scary Medusa face on to my pan with a stone. If I see any ghosts approaching, I'll hold it up to my face and make a hissing noise.

Hiss!

Decima thinks it's a stupid idea, of course. But I'm only being prepared. I bet she'll wish she'd bothered to make a ghost-frightener if we DO run into some spirits.

August IV

It was after midnight when we reached the Salt Gate. I could hear voices from deep inside the town. Ghosts? I lifted the Medusa pan to my face. Unfortunately, this made me bump into the side of the gate, so I had to lower it again.

I crept down the dark street. The houses didn't seem to have been burned at all. Maybe the damage was all on the other side of town.

We reached the road leading to the forum and I peered down it. My heart raced. There was a figure coming towards us. I lifted the pan to my face again and made a hissing noise. I could hear footsteps approaching and a ghostly laugh.

Well, it wasn't THAT ghostly, really. It was more of a giggle. I peered over the top of the pan and saw a woman pointing and laughing at me. She didn't look like a ghost, but I ran away anyway, just in case.

I caught up with Decima just in time to see
two more dark figures lurching towards us.
They didn't much look like ghosts, either.
In fact, they looked exactly like Pontius
and Spurius.

As they approached, Spurius pointed at us
and said, 'Dorkius and Decima, the children
from Rome who were eaten by the mountain
demon last week.'

Pontius smiled and waved at us.

'How are you still alive?' I asked.

'I eat plenty of fresh vegetables and take
regular exercise,' said Pontius. 'That sort
of thing.'

'But what about the lava and rocks?'
I asked.

'Never tried them,' he said. 'Is this some sort of Roman fad diet?'

I stared at Pontius in confusion. Either the poisonous gasses had warped his mind even more than usual, or there hadn't been ANY lava or rocks here. Which meant our families were safe.

I turned to Decima. 'I think we'd better check on our parents.'

She nodded and limped off down the street. I darted back home and stormed into the atrium.

'Mum! Dad!' I shouted.

I heard Dad's voice from the bedroom. 'I told you he'd come back. He always does.'

Dorky Worky, you escaped the demon!

Mum rushed out and hugged me. As soon as I could breathe, I asked her what had happened. Apparently, the tremors had continued after we'd left town, and Pontius and Pullo ordered the sacrifices to be stepped up even further.

According to Mum, this made the demon so angry he tore a hole in the mountain and made fire shoot into the sky. He farted deadly gas at Pompeii and scattered it with grey dirt. But the gods were finally satisfied with the sacrifices and they stepped in. They sent strong winds to blow the smoke and the demon away.

As for the rivers of fire, they'd all flowed down the other side of the mountain and hadn't come anywhere near Pompeii.

I tried to tell her our version of events, but she didn't want to listen. She's convinced the demon kidnapped us, so I'm not going to bother trying to tell her the truth.

I was TOTALLY starving, but all I got to eat was a plate of carrots and turnips. Apparently, all the animals have been sacrificed, so there's no meat left in town.

Mum's chickens strutted past me and clucked as I ate the boring vegetables. I wish the heat had roasted them. I could just do with a nice plate of chicken right now.

August V

Decima's parents have agreed to leave town, but mine are still refusing to go because they're CRAZY.

Mum's convinced the demon has gone and we're no longer in any danger. Dad's insisting on staying until the tax is paid. If that mountain explodes again there'll be no one left for Caesar to tax.

UPDATE

Hang on. I've just had a BRILLIANT idea to get us out of this place once and for all. I'll need Decima's help and some of her dad's things, but I think it might just work ...

August VI

After midnight, I made my way to Decima's house. She was waiting for me in the atrium with the stuff I'd asked for from her dad's room.

I'd worked out that if we both wore a wolf headdress and held candles in front of our faces, this way we would create a perfect likeness of the two-headed demon.

Well, almost perfect. Good enough for a really dark room, anyway.

We sneaked down the street to Pontius's house and found him sleeping in a bedroom off the atrium.

'Awaken!' I growled in the deepest voice I could manage and lifted the candle in front of my face. 'I am the fire demon.'

Pontius opened his eyes and screamed. 'Demon attack!' he shouted. 'Help!' He leapt out of bed and hurled a statue at us.

'Stop!' I hissed. 'You need to listen to us.'

Decima nudged me and I realized I'd forgotten to put my demon voice on.

'I mean ... do not try to call for help or I'll take over your body and control it, just like I did with that cool kid, Dorkius, from Rome.'

'Leave me in peace or I'll make the gods chase you away again,' shouted Pontius. 'Don't think I haven't prepared for this.'

'I will do you no harm,' I said. 'But first you must do something for me.'

Pontius clasped his trembling hands to his ears. 'Don't try and trick me with your clever words, demon.'

'This is no trick,' I said. 'I am making you a genuine offer.'

Pontius let his arms fall back to his sides. 'Alright. What?'

'I'll leave this town forever if you agree to pay Caesar's new tax demands with your emergency funds,' I said.

'Oh,' said Pontius, looking confused. 'I suppose we could. But why do you care? Isn't tax a bit boring for fire demons?'

'Do not question me,' I shouted. 'Or I shall aim one of my deadly farts at you.

Remember how bad they smelt when I did them on the mountain? Now imagine how bad they are close up.'

'Okay, okay, anything but THAT,' said Pontius, his eyes terrified and widening. 'I'll do anything you say.'

August VII

Pontius came round to our house today at the crack of dawn. Dad started to try and talk to him again about the taxes. But without saying a thing, Pontius plonked a bag of coins on Dad's desk, enough to pay all the tax, and then he hurried away.

Dad was so suspicious he inspected each coin before announcing the best news I've ever heard. We can go back to Rome!

Mum was really upset, which proves how bonkers she is. She'd rather stay next to a

dangerous mountain than return to the best
city in the world.

I was packed and ready in minutes, but
we couldn't go because last week Mum
gave away both our horses for sacrifice.
I can't believe she got rid of our ONLY
means of escape. She should make her silly
superstitious friends pull the wagon instead.

August VIII

Dad went to Herculaneum to buy new horses today. The only ones he could find were a pair of flea-bitten old nags that looked like they'd barely make it back to Pompeii, let alone to Rome. But he couldn't even buy those horses, because Pomponious Falto found out, and he's banned everyone from selling animals. Looks like we're stuck here after all.

UPDATE
I've just thought of something. When I was dressed as the demon, Pontius said 'Don't think I haven't prepared for this!' What if

he's been secretly storing animals in case he needs to make more sacrifices? I wouldn't put it past him.

But where would he keep them? And would they be strong enough to tow a cart all the way to Rome?

Yes   Maybe   No

August IX

I wandered around town all day trying to work out where Pontius was hiding the animals. I saw plenty of people who looked and smelled like animals, but I'm pretty sure they were all human.

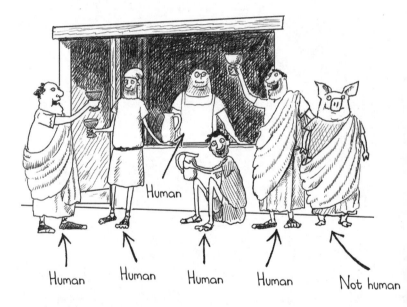

Pontius must be keeping them somewhere really secret, but where?

August X

Of course! There isn't anywhere in the town you could hide a load of animals, but there is somewhere just outside it – the fish-sauce factory. I'm off there right now to investigate. If this is the last thing I ever write, it's because I've died of foul, fishy fumes.

UPDATE
I made it to the factory. I held my breath and ventured between the rows of stinky jars. There was a large hut right at the end, so I rushed inside.

Just as I'd suspected, it was full of animals. Unfortunately, they were all pigs. I wondered if it would be possible to ride a pig all the way to Rome. I realize it wouldn't be a very dignified way to travel, but it would be better than nothing.

I was about to try sitting on one when I noticed another door at the side of the room.

I pulled it open. Ta da! There stood both of our horses. Pontius must have been holding them back in case he needed to really impress the gods.

I led them back to our house triumphantly.

UPDATE
Brilliant news. Dad has said we can leave first thing tomorrow. ROME ... I'm coming home!

August XI

We're on the way back to Rome now and that horrible mountain is almost out of sight.

I really hope it doesn't explode again. No one deserves to be swamped with liquid fire, not even the silly people of Pompeii. But I have done everything I could to warn them. If they want to risk living there, it's up to them ...

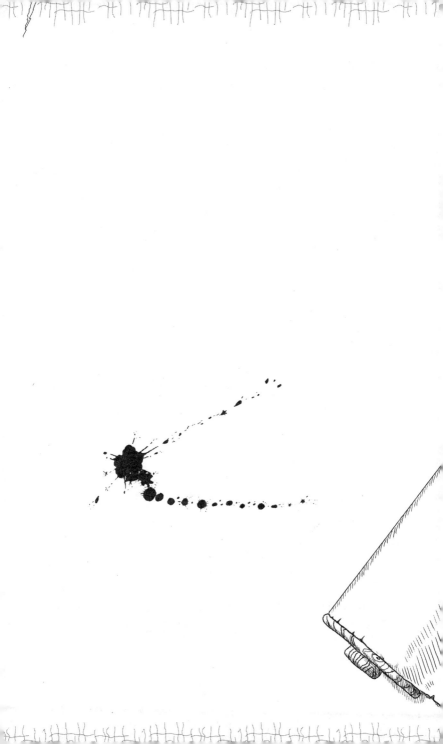

About Pompeii and Vesuvius

Dorkius wrote his scrolls in the fourth decade BC, and they're the only existing record of an eruption of Vesuvius in that era. But a much more famous one occurred over a hundred years later in AD79.

Following a series of tremors, the volcano shot millions of tonnes of lava, pumice and ash into the sky on the morning of August 24th. That night, the ash and rocks fell on Pompeii and buried two thousand people.

The town stayed buried until the middle of the eighteenth century, when excavations began and the site became a popular tourist destination.

In the nineteenth century, a man called Giuseppe Fiorelli took over. He created casts of the people who'd died by pouring plaster into the holes left by their bodies. The results were remarkably detailed, showing the straps of sandals and the fabric of tunics. One cast even showed a dog that had died struggling to free itself from its chain.

Millions of people still visit Pompeii every year to see its ruins, mosaics, wall paintings, and statues, and to get a unique glimpse into life almost two thousand years ago.

Ancient Roman Words

Dorkius's scrolls probably contain some words from Roman life that you won't know. Here are some brief explanations:

Amphitheatre – A large round structure used for gladiator fights and beast shows. The one in Pompeii could fit 20,000 people.

Atrium – The main hall of a Roman house, which led to the other rooms. Unlike today's hallways, it featured an open ceiling, a small pool and no embarrassing photos of you as a baby.

Basilisks – Legendary serpent-like creatures that could kill you just by looking at you. They don't seem to be around anymore. Maybe they all accidentally glanced in mirrors.

Caesar Cipher – A code that replaces each letter with the one three letters down the alphabet. It's named after Julius Caesar who used it in his private correspondance to protect against snoopers.

Cleopatra VII – An Egyptian queen who ruled between 51BC and 30BC. Find out what happened when Dorkius met her and her nasty brother Ptolemy in the book called *Dorkius Maximus in Egypt.*

Forum – The main square of a Roman town, which contained the temples, markets and law courts.

Freedmen – Former slaves who had been set free. Though some went on to become rich, some people still looked down on them for spending their money on tacky things.

Garum – A sauce made from fermented fish intestines that was hugely popular with many ancient Romans, but not Dorkius.

Gladiators – Ruthless fighters who were pitted against each other in huge arenas. They sometimes fought to the death, though not as often as most people think. After all, trained fighters were valuable, so why waste them willy nilly?

Gorgons – Mythical creatures with snakes for hair that could turn you to stone with a single glance. You'd be quite literally petrified if you ever saw one.

Herculaneum – A town to the west of Pompeii that was also destroyed in the volcanic eruption of AD79. The remains of some of the victims have recently been found near there, and have helped us understand more about Roman life.

Julius Caesar – A famous Roman leader with a famously silly hairstyle. Find out how Dorkius saved Caesar from assassins in *Diary of Dorkius Maximus*.

Litter – A covered chair carried by slaves that was a popular mode of transport with the rich. It would probably still be popular with the rich today if they were allowed to get away with that sort of thing.

Manticores – Legendary creatures with the body of a lion and the head of a man. Like a centaur, but much cooler.

Saturnalia – An ancient Roman celebration that took place in mid to late December, and is thought to have influenced the customs of Christmas.

Tablet – A portable writing surface made from wood covered with a layer of wax. They were eventually replaced by pens and paper. Now some people think pens and paper are about to be replaced by computer tablets, which would be fitting.

A Note On Roman Numerals

Ancient Romans didn't use the numerals we usually use today. They used a combination of the letters I, V, X, L, C, D and M. Roman numerals are still used on posh watches and movie sequels.

Here's a quick guide:

1 = I	16 = XVI	40 = XL
2 = II	17 = XVII	50 = L
3 = III	18 = XVIII	60 = LX
4 = IV	19 = XIX	100 = C
5 = V	20 = XX	200 = CC
6 = VI	21 = XXI	500 = D
7 = VII	22 = XXII	1000 = M
8 = VIII	23 = XXIII	1500 = MD
9 = IX	24 = XXIV	2000 = MM
10 = X	25 = XXV	2020 = MMXX
11 = XI	26 = XXVI	
12 = XII	27 = XXVII	
13 = XIII	28 = XXVIII	
14 = XIV	29 = XXIX	
15 = XV	30 = XXX